BUSTER
and the dandelions

By Hisako Madokoro   English text by Patricia Lantier   Illustrated by Ken Kuroi

For a free color catalog describing Gareth Stevens' list of high-quality children's books, call 1-800-341-3569 (USA) or 1-800-461-9120 (Canada).

Library of Congress Cataloging-in-Publication Data

Madokoro, Hisako, 1938-
  [Korowan to fuwafuwa. English]
  Buster and the dandelions / text by Hisako
Madokoro ; illustrations by Ken Kuroi.
    p.   cm. — (The Adventures of Buster the puppy)
  Translation of: Korowan to fuwafuwa.
  Summary: Puppy friends Buster and Snapper
venture through the meadows, blowing at dandelions
and exploring new worlds.
  ISBN 0-8368-0491-0
  [1. Dogs—Fiction. 2. Dandelions—Fiction.]
I. Kuroi, Ken, 1947- ill. II. Title. III. Series:
Madokoro, Hisako, 1938- Korowan. English.
PZ7.M2657Bu   1991
[E]—dc20
                        90-47926

North American edition first published in 1991 by
Gareth Stevens Children's Books
1555 North RiverCenter Drive, Suite 201
Milwaukee, Wisconsin 53212, USA

This U.S. edition copyright © 1991. Text copyright
© 1991 by Gareth Stevens, Inc. First published as
Korowan To Fuwafuwa (*Korowan and the
Dandelions*) in Japan with an original copyright
© 1988 by Hisako Madokoro (text) and Ken Kuroi
(illustrations). English translation rights arranged
with CHILD HONSHA through Japan Foreign-
Rights Centre.

Cover design: Kristi Ludwig

Printed in the United States of America

1 2 3 4 5 6 7 8 9 97 96 95 94 93 92 91

Gareth Stevens Children's Books
MILWAUKEE

2

Hundreds of dandelions grew in Buster's back yard. Buster liked to make the parachutes fly into the air.

"Wheee! This is fun!"

Buster's friend Snapper ran over to join the game.

"Come play with the parachutes!" said Buster.

The two little puppies
played happily in the
dandelion patch.

Buster wagged his tail with
glee. "Let's find more
flowers!" he said.

Buster and Snapper raced
into a large field.

"Look! There are dandelions
everywhere. See all the little
parachutes floating in the air!"

Beyond a narrow stream
were more and more
dandelions.

"Let's go!" said Snapper, and
he jumped over the water.

"Wait a minute!" cried Buster. "I'm not so sure I can jump over this stream."

His legs were shaking. The water was very cold. Buster was worried.

"Come on!" said Snapper.
Buster looked carefully at
the water.

"Ready . . . Set . . ."

"GO!"

Snapper cheered as Buster
sailed over the stream right
into a dandelion patch.

"I did it! I did it!" Buster
cried out happily.

19

Buster and Snapper ran
all around the field of
dandelions. Parachutes
flew everywhere.

Buster and Snapper ran
all around the field of
dandelions. Parachutes
flew everywhere.

It was getting darker. Buster
and Snapper jumped easily
over the stream as they ran
toward home.

23

"Good night, Snapper," said Buster. "See you tomorrow."

As white parachutes floated in the air, Buster watched his little friend walk home.

24